Brookhaven

David Royce

Published by David Royce, 2025.

COPYRIGHT

Copyright © 2025 David Royce. All Rights Reserved.No part of this publication may be reproduced, distributed, or transmitted in any form or by any means, including photocopying, recording, or other electronic or mechanical methods, without the prior written permission of the author, except in the case of brief quotations embodied in critical reviews and certain other noncommercial uses permitted by copyright law. For permission requests, please contact the author at davidroyceauthor@gmail.com.

This book is a work of fiction. Names, characters, businesses, places, events, and incidents are either the products of the author's imagination or used in a fictitious manner. Any resemblance to actual persons, living or dead, or actual events is purely coincidental.

CHAPTER 1

Walking down the halls of Brookhaven was like walking down the corridor to death's door. At least that's what Chrissy (with two S's) thought. They used to call these places *old folks homes*. Later, they changed it to *retirement homes*. But now they were regulated to *assisted nursing facilities*.

Didn't matter to Chrissy. She got paid the same no matter what you wanted to call a place that housed the *elderly* patients, so close to the grave that they were practically slow walking stiffs as soon as they arrived.

No matter how you said it, this was the last junction for old people. That's how it is though. This is a dumping ground for the least worthy of society. Just like you would dump a mattress that had seen better days off in the trash. It had it's use but it's someone else's problem now.

Chrissy was fine with that, and had been for the past three years. She did her duty with precision and attention to detail. She'd been puked on, grabbed, choked, and been present for the eventual deaths of the residents. *Just another day. Just another old person going to the great beyond.* She told herself this but, deep down, she was never ready for what her rounds at Brookhaven brought.

Despite what the movies and TV shows told you about these places, you couldn't actually imagine what really took place. Chrissy had walked in on Tom Peterson beating his meat like it owed him money. She'll never forget what an eighty seven year old man looks like as he masturbates.

Stan Jameson and Claire Horthawn (eighty one and ninety respectively) doing the nasty deed, their colostomy bags banging a tune on the sides of their handrails in time to their wrinkled love making, would forever be etched in her mind.

And Peter Strome (seventy nine) snorting what looked an awful lot like cocaine from his desk with a rolled up dollar bill would give her nightmares.

But Chrissy was fine with all of this. *What are you gonna do? People fuck, people do drugs, people are animals no matter their age,* she thought. She did her due diligence every night, round after round.

It wasn't until she entered the room of Alice Walker, ninety three, that she doubted her job. Sex, drugs, and jerking off was one thing. No problemo. A-OK even. But *this…*

Alice Walker (maiden name Seares) had led a good life, all things considered. She was an original settler and married young to an older man named Delbert Walker, a lawyer by trade but a philanderer and miscreant by nature. Her life with him wasn't necessarily happy but not completely shit so she stayed with him until his untimely death from a heart attack at age sixty seven. Truth be told, she was happy when death came calling for him. He had five other children with just as many women that she was aware of. Probably more but she had no way to prove that.

Delbert was a man full of sin but he was also very good at business. He owned a chain of porn theaters and money came from all directions (as did the people who frequented his theaters). Delbert and Alice never had children together but that was fine with Alice. When he died, there was nobody to share his wealth with and Alice had enough to live comfortably.

She took her inheritance and moved to Joring Michigan, a town that accepted her with open arms. She dated again, started her life over again, and didn't regret her past.

Chrissy really liked Alice Walker. Alice was always kind and almost never needed her assistance in cleaning or eating. *A good egg. An independent woman who just happened to lose her way in the latter stage of her life.*

This is the thought that would stay with her when Chrissy walked into Alice's room on February 12th 2023.

CHAPTER 2

Blood. Lots of it too. The windows, the door, the floor. There wasn't a surface that was once painted white unaffected by the crimson. Chrissy first took in the scene, eyes darting back and forth like they were two swinging lanterns in the night. She *wanted* to act professional. She *wanted* to pretend that this was a perfectly normal thing. Instead, she screamed.

A not *professional* thing to do but what other reaction could possibly have been appropriate? The body of Alice Walker was desecrated, as Chrissy would tell anybody who listened later. Others would use phrases like *flayed, gutted, and massacred* but Chrissy would only think of this as a desecration.

Alice's body laying in her bed, cut open from neck to navel. Her intestines spread like a spider in eight different directions. Her heart was missing from where it should have been but placed on her forehead.

Chrissy let her screams out and then some. She was only halfway through her shift.

CHAPTER 3

Things are different now, Stephanie Sawyer thought. She walked up to the second floor of Brookhaven and made her way to the nurses station. She didn't need anyone to tell her something was going on since she could see the police and ambulance guys hanging around but she figured she better check in anyway.

The night nurse, Marge Ekelson, greeted her by waving her hands and stepping out from behind the desk.

"It's so awful", Marge said, "there's blood everywhere. Looks like someone butchered her. It's just..." Marge broke down.

Stephanie walked past, giving Marge a nod. Whatever was going on here, she needed to reserve her strength. She saw the police and medics but focused on Chrissy, sitting on a bench outside of the room, sullen and unmistakably traumatized.

"Hey, girl." she said, not really knowing what to say, yet better than nothing. Stephanie rubbed Chrissy's back, unsure of what to do given the circumstances. She looked at Chrissy and saw a person that was broken.

"I'll take it from here, no worries ", Stephanie said. With no response from Chrissy except for a shudder, she walked into the room that once belonged to Alice Walker.

CHAPTER 4

Mrs. Delphine Hardwick toked until her face turned almost purple. She slowly exhaled the smoke and offered it to Gabe Albright.

"NO THANKS", he yelled as he always does, "I DON'T WANNA GET HIGH. ALICE IS DEAD".

Gabe is deaf and always yells even when he thinks he's being quiet. He was in *god damn VIETNAM* and figured the world owed him something even if he was just an officer that never saw the first sign of combat.

"GIMME MY JUICE", he said. By "juice", he means Wild Turkey. Delphine flips him off, "Take what I give ya or go and fuck yourself", she says. Gabe's face scrunches up.

There's a lockdown. Not a standard one. Generally when one of the *walking dead* (as they've all come to think of themselves) dies, they have to sit in their rooms and *reflect* on what happened. Gabe thinks this is dumb. He's ninety years old and doesn't need the drama. This lockdown is more intense. They were locked in their rooms like prisoners and he didn't like that one bit.

Sure, Alice was dead. Hell, she was carved up like a turkey on Thanksgiving at the hand of Michael J. Fox. That didn't mean he had to suffer the indignity for it though. *Goddamn fascists.*

But, despite Delphine's harshness when offering the joint, he does want to get high or drunk, to feel *something*.

He accepts grudgingly, but he tokes deep, knowing that the good Lord above has his back. "PISS AND FIRE", he says. It's his favorite expression when something goes wrong as if yelling this phrase makes everything alright. Delphine only responds with a snort.

"You can barely piss anymore and the only fire you have comes from that rot gut you call whiskey", she says.

Gabe takes a long drag and holds it in as long as his deteriorating lungs can handle before blowing the smoke out with a coughing fit that would normally alert the medical staff.

"WANNA FUCK?", he yells.

Delphine gets red in the face. She's actually pretty disgusted by Gabe but, she had to admit, the man was hung like a torpedo. She gives him an unsteady glare and shushes him. "You need to leave my room. Get out", she says. She actually wants to bang Gabe but he's being much too loud about it and she has a fine respectable Southern Belle reputation to uphold.

Gabe looks at her kind of funny and yells "GOUT? I DON'T HAVE THE GOUT".

Delphine shakes her head and takes back the joint.

CHAPTER 5

Three days later seems like a lifetime because, at their age, three days could actually *be* a lifetime. But the residents of Brookhaven get back into their daily routines and nobody mentions Alice Walker. There are now forty four full time inhabitants left and life is too precious to focus on the dead.

Unless your name is Winona B. Nobody except staff and medical personnel knows what the "B" stands for. Gabe thinks it's BITCH because she's one of the very few females here who refuse his advances. *Beaufort, Belmont,* and *Barry* have been mentioned but who knows for sure?

Winona is between ninety eight and one hundred and five, her age being just as much of a mystery as her Christian name. The only black person at Brookhaven, she has done her best to avoid the verbal pitfalls of racism from the others who claim *I'm not racist. It was just a different time when I was growing up.*

Bullshit and excuses, she thought. As if, at some point in their lives, the others experienced the violence of the civil rights movement and just threw their hands up in the air and decided *afro American* or *negro* was not as offensive as the *N-WORD*. Like they just took the least offensive (but still offensive nonetheless) terminology and cemented in their minds that this was acceptable.

Why not just *friend* or *person*? She might be as old as Moses but Gabe could go fuck himself when he said he wanted some *brown sugar*. And, she swears, if Daphne Salsbury asks to touch her hair just *one more time,* there was going to be trouble.

As Winona laboriously made her way down the hallway, she put all that aside in her mind. Death was a common accurance here but this sort of brutality was different. They needed to band together because if this kind of thing happened to one of them it could happen again. And she's seen enough horror movies in her life to know that the *black character* always gets killed off quick.

Not today, motherfuckers, not today, she thought. And she would be right as it turns out. Because a very white, very racist, and very despicable man would soon realize that dealing drugs was not worth the cost.

CHAPTER 6

Danny Melcroft punched into his shift at Brookhaven just as he always did. He considers himself a *medical staff member* but his training mainly consisted of emptying bedpans and mopping up leftovers from meal time after the old folks had eaten and pissed themselves. The money he made from his paycheck was shit, but there's more than one way to skin a wrinkly cat, wasn't there?

Forget about the nickel and dime stuff when he slid the dollar bills from their drawers after lights out. These people here *loved* their drugs and he always came fully loaded with as much as they wanted. Percocet, Vicodan, weed, shrooms, cocaine, ketamine, and morphine were his trade. *A buck was a buck and a fuck was a fuck* was his motto.

He whistled as he walked up to the second floor. After the old broad was gutted, he figured this would be a fine day to unload his inventory on the rest of the skeleton crew. He whistled, he walked, and entered the common area.

Who the fuck is this. A darkie? He'd never seen a black person here, and he thought that was all the better. But there she sat as if she belonged there. He made a point of walking close to her and scowling. She looked him in the eye and flipped him off. *I'm gonna slap that look right off your face, he thought* before turning to *his* people.

"I have all the magic pills, tokes, and snorts you need", he announced, "first come, first serve". He reached into his backpack and came out with a rainbow of pharmaceuticals that would make a drugstore blush.

This is the point where these fossils are practically clawing at each other to get what they want. Violent at times but a very slow meandering violence since their average speed was slow to lethargic. At their age, a good shit could cause permanent damage.

Yet they didn't move. Barely noticed him. He tried to look in their eyes but their attention was elsewhere. They were all looking at that...*black* woman. What the hell? *She* didn't have high quality (yet illegally obtained) drugs. *She* didn't come in every shift and make an extra three hundred dollars. And *she* was black!

At that point, Danny Melcroft stuffed the drugs back into his bag and slammed the door on his way out. *How dare they treat me like this. After everything I've done for them?"*

He fumes as he walks to the locker room. He approaches his locker and throws his backpack inside. *That BITCH. That black bitch cost me three hundred dollars.* Now what was he going to do? Just work his normal shift for shit pay? He was contemplating this when the lights went out.

He would never admit it to anyone even if he would have lived but he let out a little whimper. He let his eyes adjust to the darkness, cursing the cheap bastards that ran the place. Danny stands up and feels his way along the wall for the door. Inch by inch, he slowly makes his way to what he thinks is the exit. Shuffling and wary, he heads toward the door.

He sees light coming in from underneath the exit. He has an opportunity to feel the slightest bit of relief until the light is gone, replaced by a shadow. The darkness is almost smothering. Almost. The door bursts open.

The glint of a knifes edge and the sound of that knife hissing through the air until it punctures his flesh is all he sees and hears. It's introducing itself to him.

They meet with a force that defies logic. The knife punctures, rips, and shreds. Danny screams, unheard, and the rendering of skin and what lies beneath are the only sounds if anyone were listening. But, of course, they weren't. Because Danny is...was...an asshole.

CHAPTER 7

Stephanie has had a rough couple of days. After the Alice Walker incident (all death, no matter how grisly, is always just an incident) she did her best to comfort Chrissy. Woman to woman, caretaker to caretaker. She knew it didn't accomplish anything though. Chrissy was lost in her own head, a world where someone could just walk into an assisted care facility and have their way at dismemberment without interruption. In Chrissy's new inner world, there wasn't good and evil. Just evil and more evil.

Even though she said she'd be back after some time off, Stephanie knew better. Chrissy would be running forever, away from Joring Michigan and especially away from Brookhaven. Yet there wasn't an amount of distance that would stop the nightmares.

For her own part, Stephanie had kept it together mostly. The yellow police tape was still across the door of Alice Walker's room but she steeled herself for the day when it was removed and they would have to deep clean it to make space for another resident. Business was business.

Walking in to her shift that day she noticed Danny Melcroft's truck still in the parking lot. *Strange,* she thought, *he's always the first one out.* She didn't like Danny and always tried to be wherever he wasn't when they worked the same shift. He was one of those people that got on everybody's bad side sooner or later. Racist as shit and only thinking about himself. She hoped he hadn't worked overtime because she couldn't stand the sight of him.

She would really hate the sight of him even more when she entered the employee locker room.

Danny's body swung from two hooks, each one inserted into both sides of his temple with the other ends attached to the metal locker doors. His arms were splayed out like Jesus at the crucifixion but his insides were nothing but a pile of viscera at his feet. Flies had found their home and the stench of decay assaulted Stephanie like a physical attack.

His heart had been placed at his feet.

It was at that moment Stephanie knew she would be joining Chrissy. Her already frazzled nerves had reached a breaking point of no return. Her stomach churned. All of the overpriced coffee and egg with sausage breakfast sandwich became a sickly grey goop on the floor as it spewed from her mouth with her body closely following it's descent.

When she could finally breathe again she looked up at Danny's body. A dog to its vomit. Why was he swinging? The chains that held him in place clanked against the locker doors. Was he...*could* he still be alive? That was her final thought before a dark shape entered her vision. The last thing she ever remembered is the blade across her throat.

CHAPTER 8

"I'M NOT RACIST", Gabe yells, "I VOTED FOR OSAMA".

"*Obama*, you damned fool", Delphine corrects him.

Gabe raises his hands in protest, "THAT'S WHAT I SAID. THE BLACK FELLA".

Winona shakes her head but keeps quiet. She's pretty sure they're playing the game of *who is the least racist* because she's there. White people feel the need to go overboard in showing how *not* racist they are in the presence of a black person. She let's it go because there are more important things to focus on right now.

The bodies of Stephanie Sawyer and Danny Melcroft were discovered just hours ago. The police were swarming the grounds like a group of angry fire ants and the residents were all placed in a tight lockdown inside of the dining room, which was really nothing more than a large area with tables that resembled the chow hall of a modern prison.

Every few minutes another contrived empathetic voice sing-songed through the room's speaker reminding them that, should there be some kind of emergency, they should pick up the emergency phone immediately.

Delphine holds the joint she just rolled and lights up. The smell of marijuana fills the air but nobody complains. Why would they? The general consensus among the long timers at Brookhaven was simply *why not?*

When you're young and starting your quest through life, you try to fit the pieces together. Career, marriage, children, grandkids, a house, a car, and friends. You struggle to make those pieces fit yet, after that final piece is put in place, you find yourself relegated to a place like Brookhaven.

The only goal left is simply to die.

So *why not* try all the drugs? *Why not* get laid every chance you can? After all, every day you're alive and wake up feeling blessed because you've survived another day is just another day that brings you closer to death and whatever lies beyond. You can't escape that fact no matter how much philosophy you subscribe to.

Winona, Gabe, Delphine, and others sit at the table and contemplated this as the joint is passed. Except for Eric Ogborn. He takes this as a sin and yells at the others.

"Ye sinners who worship the needs of the flesh shall perish in the hellfire that our Lord God has created for you".

"Shut up, Eric, your God has failed", Winona said. She looked him in the eyes, her own eyes pillars of fire. Eric shut up even though his jaw continued working as if he was trying to come up with words.

Eric was ninety one years old and his legacy was one of religious intolerance. *How dare she speak to a man of God like this,* he thought. Words failed him for the first time but he wagged a finger at them and walked to the door. He forgot that they were locked in and, when he attempted to open the door with a righteous fury, his hand slipped off the knob and he tumbled backward to the floor. Something cracked in his body that sounded like a gunshot in the cavernous room.

As Delphine and Winona made their way over to him, he suddenly sat up. His eyes which once glowed with nothing but religious zeal darkened. His curt slit of a mouth grinned so wide that he appeared to be the Joker to anyone's Batman. And then he ran across the room and bounded up the wall to the uppermost window by the kitchen, shattering it as he flung himself through.

"Did you see that"?, Delphine asked to no one in particular.

"I DID", said Gabe, "HE'S KINDA QUEER ISN'T HE"?

"*Shut up, Gabe*", came everyone's reply at the same time.

CHAPTER 9

Eric dropped to the ground and entered Brookhaven through the delivery door. He wandered the halls with his newfound strength and mobility. He hasn't felt this alive in so many years. He could run without a limp, he was agile, and his thoughts...oh, his *thoughts,* were clear and vivid. He would bring the next biblical plague to these sinners. And Evelyn Masters needed him. He would not disappoint.

CHAPTER 10

Evelyn Masters (aged seventy nine) stayed in her room through all of this *nonsense* as she called it. She was perfectly happy at Brookhaven. Her bedding was cleaned, her meals were served, and she was content with that. All that talk of murder was just leftist bullshit as far as she was concerned and she knew her great President, Donald himself, would not let her down. An American flag waved as proudly as the Confederate flag right beside her window and nobody could tell her they weren't both the same.

Thankfully, she'd been spared from this unconstitutional lockdown. She realised that the *mainstream media* had manipulated a couple of deaths and, of course, came up with a doomsday scenario. She wouldn't have any of that and refused to go into a lockdown (because that's what *they* wanted).

When her door was kicked in she assumed that Joe Biden, the *unelected* President had finally found a way to get to her. *Just like a libtard* she thought. Instead, the Reverend Eric loomed in her doorway. She grabbed her chest in relief.

"I knew this was bullshit, pardon my French, but I'm glad you're here Reverend. Did you know that they let a *colored* woman in here? Probably one of those illegals. They always sneak in right under your nose and..."

But the good Reverend Eric wasn't listening. He wasn't even looking at her so much as *through* her. He sniffed the room and, in two strides, planted himself on top of Evelyn. *Doesn't he have hip dysplasia?*, she thought.

She screamed. Eric smiled but his body started convulsing. She could feel his trembling and didn't know what to think of it.

Then, Eric exploded. His remains were on the walls, ceilings, and floor. There was nothing left but pulpy bloody remnants.

But in his place, a dark figure sat on her legs. A mirthless smile spread across the face and the blade went to town.

CHAPTER 11

The sounds of activity in the hallway had the group straining their ears and sitting to attention inside of the dining area. At first there were screams followed by heavy running footsteps and people barking out commands. But it was the gunshots followed by even more screams that had them all staring at each other with eyes as big as saucers.

Winona was the first to walk to the door. She twisted the knob but it was still locked. She feebly pounded on it, willing someone to respond, but she was met with dying screams and the sound of panic. Whatever was happening out there must be horrible because it seemed that they were all but forgotten.

And they were trapped.

Delphine was already at the emergency phone because this situation absolutely constituted an emergency. But all she heard on the other end was static. She saw Winona looking at her and she put the phone in its cradle, shaking her head no.

They both made their way back to the table, each of them trying to figure out what was going on. "Hey", Delphine said, "where's Gabe?" Winona stared at the empty seat and thought that wherever Gabe went, it wasn't a good idea to be alone right now.

"C'mon, let's get the old bastard back here", she said.

CHAPTER 12

Mildred Halsey, aged eighty two, was a soft spoken woman these days. She used most of her words and energy when she was young, being a dominatrix at an exclusive underground nightclub in New Jersey for the best years of her life. She'd spanked more behinds than a Catholic kindergarten class and handcuffed more men than the police department. She was aged out of that scene because, after a certain point, a wrinkly old woman in black spandex with a ball gag didn't really have the desired effect any longer.

So Mildred (or *Mistress Milly*) just kept to herself for the most part. Brookhaven, to her, provided a little taste of the life she'd once led. Men never stopped fantasizing and, even though it wasn't like back in her heyday, she still received monthly visits from her *grandsons,* as the staff were led to believe. What they did in the privacy of her own room was none of their business though.

It's not like she avoided the other residents here, but she didn't need their drugs to get by. Young people these days came with a supply that would make Scarface blush. They gave her more than enough and they didn't need a little blue pill to get to the point either.

Viagra day at Brookhaven was like Christmas to a toddler. Everyone, men and women alike, shuffled around with smiles and the staff had a lot more sheets to change and clean.

Most people didn't realize she was in the same room, as quiet as she was, which is why none of the others noticed her missing from her seat along with Gabe.

Gabe had slowly made his way into the main kitchen while the two women were busy with the door and phone. She followed because she figured a snack was in order considering how the group was simply left locked up like prisoners.

This would save Gabe's life, as it turned out, but Mildred would never be the same again.

CHAPTER 13

Gabe's eyes were wide and a smile crossed his crusty face as he stared at the sight in front of him. The commercial sized refrigerator and freezer stood open in front of him, filled with everything that made life worth living.

Except for pussy and beer, he reminded himself. Still, the goopy, sometimes tasteless gruel the residents had to live on was an outright slap to the face considering the contents in front of his eyes.

Ham, thick cut pork chops, pizza rolls, strip steaks, french fries, frozen meatballs and pizzas, and potato salad all basked in the glorious light of the bulb. Gabe barely had time to realise that the staff used the resident's money to purchase this for themselves while serving him and the others the minimum ingredients just so they didn't die.

Ha! Lock me up, will ya? I'm gonna eat until someone stops me or my heart gives out, you greedy assholes, Gabe thought as he reached in for the potato salad. As his mind raced with the possibilities of devouring several greasy pork chops to go with the mustardy cholesterol drenched potatoes, the heavy door of the refrigerator slammed into his arm. A crack echoed and Gabe finally had a reason to scream as his arm shattered like the dreams of a runaway landing in Hollywood.

He dropped to the kitchen floor as a dark shape stood towering over him. A knife was raised and started its descent. Gabe put up his one good hand defensively.

"Hey, fuckface, leave him alone", Mildred shouted. The figure froze mid strike and stared at the intruder. A shadowy sneer crossed what passed for a face and glided over to her in seconds. She picked up the rolling pin and swung for the bleachers. Her aim was off and missed as the figure swung the blade downward and off came three of her fingers. Blood jettisoned from the stubs as the rolling pin dropped to the floor and rolled away.

Mildred shrieked until her lungs were dust as she tried to staunch the bleeding. Gabe crawled over to her, his one arm a broken mess. They wildly looked around but no signs of another presence was to be found.

Gabe carefully used his good arm to grab the counter and pull himself up to a standing position. He looked Mildred in the eye.

"REALLY? YOU MISSED?"

Mildred passed out.

CHAPTER 14

Delphine and Winona held onto each other as they made their way back to the kitchen. Glass from the window Reverend Eric had jumped through crunched beneath their slippers. Delphine stopped short, pulling Winona back.

"Something's not right about all this", she said.

"Nothing's been right for a long time here, girl. Evil always finds its place back", Winona replied. And she knew evil when she saw it. Growing up, Winona had been privy to certain ceremonies and rituals. Her mother was a well respected practitioner of hoodoo. She would break the hexes and curses of the voodoo clans. Bring back peace and hope to those under the spells of dark magic.

Delphine looked at Winona and gave her arm a squeeze. "You're talking about Dennis Forth, aren't you?"

Dennis Forth was the man who opposed the building of this facility on what he said was sacred pagan land. Before he was run over by a very drunk mailman and died underneath a pile of junk mail, he claimed to any and all that would listen that this piece of real estate belonged to him and his family. It was said to actually be a cult that practiced blood rituals under the guise of paganism.

The county, however, disagreed. This wasn't a Native American burial ground and it wasn't a place that was cursed by witches or had any other significant curses laid upon it. As far as they were concerned, pagan land disputes were regulated to the same place that Bigfoot and alien sightings were disputed. That would be online forums and Facebook hoax sites. But, according to the county, this was a perfectly insignificant piece of land to build a *retirement care facility* on.

So, they did. And even though they were wrong, they wouldn't admit their mistake until long after the bodies had been recovered and after any statute of limitations laws passed. No need for lawsuits. What's done is done after all.

But Dennis Forth remembered. Even in his grave. There was no time limit on revenge and he would have his.

CHAPTER 15

Delphine and Winona stared into each other's eyes. Winona hated to admit it but Delphine was exactly on point. She never thought a proper country bred woman such as Delphine would have any clue about Dennis Forth or his plan of revenge.

"Yes. I'm talking about Dennis", Winona admitted. "He was an awful man even when he was alive. But in his death, after this structure was built, he...", she didn't know how to continue.

Any words she thought of sounded like the ramblings of a crazy person. And that was kind of fitting. Because *if* they were found and *if* they were rescued, what would they say happened here? A wayward ghost exacting his revenge? *Just the imaginations of the elderly,* people would say. Nobody believes old folks or kids.

"He came back to kill us", Delphine finished for her, not a cloud of doubt in her eye. Winona nodded wearily. A scream and a sound like a package of meat hitting the floor made them both turn to the kitchen. Their eyes met again and they gave each other a slight nod before heading off to investigate the strange sound, both knowing full well that's how people die in a horror movie. But onward they walked.

They edged around the corner and saw Mildred with her hand to her chest, spewing blood, and Gabe standing with one arm that was bent at an almost impossible angle. Gabe was moaning but Mildred was in shock, staring at her hand as if it was an alien from outer space.

They moved as quickly as they could to the carnage and separated to different victims. Winona put her arm around Gabe's waist, supporting him with all that was left of her strength. He grunted and said, "I WANT MY JUICE."

"Yeah, honey, we all want our juice", Winona answered as she guided him from the kitchen.

Delphine took Mildred in her arms and grabbed a kitchen towel from the counter, wrapping it around the hand that once held all five digits. "You'll be okay, you'll be fine", she kept saying. Maybe it was for Mildred or maybe just for herself, but she kept the mantra flowing as she led Mildred back into the dining hall.

The foursome made their way back into the dining area and collapsed once they did. Mildred was still bleeding but not as much. Whether that was a good or bad thing, Delphine didn't know. Gabe seemed to be okay despite his obvious discomfort, his arm like an impressionist painting, and Winona seemed winded but otherwise fine.

None of them spoke as they caught their breath. Winona looked around at the carnage and, considering what they heard earlier, realised that the situation had pretty much left them on their own.

"We need to find a way out of here", she said, "Things are going on that nobody will believe but if we stay in here, we'll just be victims."

Gabe raised his head and gave her a look of confusion. "WHY NOT JUST USE THE EMERGENCY DOOR IN THE BACK?"

"There's a door in the back?" Delphine asked.

"THERE'S ALWAYS A DOOR IN THE BACK", Gabe said, "I LEARNED THAT FROM MY SEX LIFE".

"Shut up, Gabe", the rest said in unison.

CHAPTER 16

Captain Bruce Gillis received the first call from Brookhaven and dismissed it as a prank. *God damn kids and their interwebs bullshit. Multiple murders? A killer on the loose?* Had to be a prank. He'd been the Captain of the Floring police for more years than Carter had pills and he wasn't going to waste his, or his deputies, time with the wasteful bullshit of this generation.

But when the second call came, followed by the third, fourth, and seemingly beyond infinity of ringing phones, he sent every deputy he had at his disposal out to the old folks home. And now, *this*.

Bruce grabbed his gear and headed out the door. That gear included a long barrel .45 Magnum that would put a hole through a wall a hundred feet away and turn any body in its way into human paste. So he wasn't worried.

It was only when he arrived at Brookhaven and walked inside that he immediately regretted ever getting into law enforcement. The floor was red. At first, he thought that red was a weird color for the floors of an old folks home. But as he stepped further, the metallic smell filled his nostrils and the squelch under his boots made him realize that something was very very off about this place. The floors weren't red, they were covered in blood.

He slowly made his way past the reception area to the main hallway. In his years of providing protection and service to the fine people of Joring Michigan he thought he'd seen everything. A drunk that had passed out on the street being run over by a garbage truck, a meth head so violent he had slit his own neck, and even a six year old girl who, for some fucked up reason or another, had killed her own parents. Life was full of tragedy.

But this scene before him was by far the worst. *So many body parts* he thought. Arms, legs, heads, torsos. They were all spread throughout the hallway in no discernible order. There wasn't any recognition between them.

The coroner's gonna have a hard time with this, was his first thought. He did recognise the uniform pieces attached to the limbs. His deputies. This wasn't a murder, this was a slaughter. Bruce pulled his weapon from his holster and made his way down the hall.

Most of the doors he opened revealed nothing but more carnage and his stomach was little more than putty in his body. *Yes, I'm gonna lose it. I'm gonna vomit so hard that I can't tell which guts are mine and which are my deputies.*

A high pitched alarm went through his head just as he was at his breaking point. At first he attributed this to his mental state. Finding the desecrated remains of your co-workers and friends could do that to a man. But then he realised that he was hearing an alarm from an emergency door opening.

Someone had to open that door. With renewed, though not quite full, strength, Bruce headed toward the sound.

CHAPTER 17

When Gabe pushed on the door handle with his good arm an alarm started ringing out. They all covered their ears but stumbled out into the outer area of Brookhaven. The grounds weren't so bad. A man-made pond took up most of the back but woods surrounded them on every side.

Delphine closed the door and, thankfully, the alarm stopped shrieking. Standing there, nobody had a clue where to go next.

"I think it's this way", Mildred said. Her stubs that were once fingers seemed to be okay now but she was looking awfully pale, especially in the moonlight. She was trying to point but her nubs were not exactly clear.

"I'VE GOT THIS", Gabe said. He positioned himself in front of the others and tenderly held his shattered arm in his other hand.

"I GOTTA TELL YA, I THINK MOST OF YOU ARE PUSSIES. I THINK MOST OF YOU WOULD ROLL OVER QUICKER THAN A STRAY DOG WOULD ROLL OVER FOR A CHICKEN BONE. BUT I REFUSE TO DIE TONIGHT. NOW, I NEED MY JUICE. WHO'S WITH ME?"

Not exactly a motivational speech that would be remembered in history books but it had the desired effect all the same.

Winona walked to his side. "And I need my spell books"

Delphine followed suit. "And I need my weed and nunchucks".

Mildred was the last. "And I need my fingers back. But, since that ain't gonna happen, I need my whip".

With declarations all around, they headed to the door around the side of the building that led them back to their rooms.

CHAPTER 18

We can't walk through this was Delphine's first thought. Their small but determined group had made their way back into the building. But the hallways were covered in carnage. Everyone stood where they entered, each one considering the best course of action, but Gabe finally moved forward. "I'M GETTING MY JUICE", he said more to himself than anybody else.

He tried to avoid the piles of limbs and human offal as best as he could, yet he almost spilled forward on a pile of intestines seeping out from one of the bodies.

"GODDAMN GUTS ARE LIKE ICE", he bellowed.

The others followed, arm in arm, none of them looking downward. The smell was bad enough without the visuals. They finally made it to the stairs, which were thankfully clean of viscera.

Once they reached the top, they separated and proceeded to their rooms. They would fight this evil on *their* terms and accept the consequences either way. They might be old but they had a lot of fight in them.

But, still, they *were* old and not all of them could hope to survive what was to come. Hope was a dangerous thing after a certain age. Cynicism, withdrawal, and acceptance of death were the currencies of the elderly. Hope was a young person's game. But, to the old man and old women's credit, they determined to end this nightmare one way or another. God help anyone that stood in their way.

CHAPTER 19

Bruce Gillis moved with a purpose towards the noisy alarm. He was quickly out of breath since he hasn't needed to move with anything resembling quickness for many years. He felt the sweat forming in his armpits and along his back but was determined to find any survivors.

The alarm suddenly stopped its racket and the utter silence made him sweat even more. It had been coming from the dining area, of this he was certain. The door was locked from the outside and no matter how many times he kicked it, there was no way past this barrier. Unless...

He looked down at the body parts that seemed to come from a horrific fever dream. Among the slaughter, he saw the torso of one of the nurses. *She was a pretty thing,* he thought. He allowed himself a brief moment to reflect on the life that could have been for the young lady before reaching into the pockets of her uniform. Blood covered his hand as he dug around to locate what he needed.

Keys. Bruce held them up before his eyes and stood up. He placed one of the keys in the lock of the dining room and the familiar *click* gave him some hope. He opened the door quickly, gun at the ready, and unsteadily made a sweep of the main dining area.

It was not only clear but silent. Some of the chairs were out of place which let him know that someone had been in here recently. He made his way to the back, turning his head from side to side as if he were waiting for something to jump out at him. The only sound was his boot steps until the crunching noise made him jump a little. Looking down, he noticed the glass under his feet. Up above, a window that had clearly been breached in some form or another.

Something was off though. Judging by the small amount of broken shards on the inside, he knew that the breach had come from the inside to the outside. And that didn't ease his nervousness one bit because it would be impossible for a person to do that. Even a young, athletic, flexible man or woman couldn't have defied gravity enough to get up there from down here.

Bruce turned to walk into the kitchen and noticed the mess. Some food strewn about the floor by the refrigerator and, just before that, blood. A good amount that spread in streaks which meant someone had either wiped at it or was dragged through it. He bent over and saw several tiny sausages scattered among the blood trail. *Never seen sausages like this before* he thought as he reached down to pick one up.

His hand stopped short just in time as his brain kicked in screaming *Fingers. Those aren't sausages. They're human fingers.* His heartbeat dialed up from an eleven to a twenty and the gun felt like a hundred pound weight in his hand. He used the counter to haul himself back to his feet. There was only one place left to go here, the emergency exit beyond the refrigerator. It was only about twenty feet in front of him but it might as well have been on the other side of the city. His heart was racing, his head was pounding, and he felt as useless as a plate of bacon at a kosher wedding.

The alarm. It came from this door. Someone had just used it. At least his mind was still working somewhat reasonably. Summoning all the courage he could gather, he started towards the exit and into the unknown.

CHAPTER 20

Each of the residents had their secrets. Hidden things that the staff would never allow were tucked away in false bottoms of trunks, the back areas of closets (well disguised by clothes, books, and bags), and even taped securely underneath furniture where eyes never looked.

Delphine sat on the end of her bed and lit the small bong that she didn't really have to hide at all. It sat on a shelf along with various other knick knacks when not in use and nobody had ever paid any attention to it.

She drags deep, feeling the smoke burn her lungs before exhaling slowly. Her and Winona had talked about the pagan curse and how to stop it. Delphine wanted to grab her nunchucks but knew it wouldn't do any good to fight what they were facing. Still, having them in her hands would be comforting.

Winona had acted nervous but confident as they all separated. Maybe she knew something? Maybe she had a plan? Delphine dismissed this thought at first glance but, the more she toked, it kind of made sense. Winona seemed to know all about the curse and the land the building was built on. She also came from a line of folks who practiced some sort of magik and that was a thousand percent more than all of the

others combined.

Delphine decided she would trust Winona. Whatever it was she was planning would be more useful than a set of numchucks in the hands of an old woman who was as high as the stars above. She chuckled to herself at the thought of her swinging that weapon and accidentally cracking herself in the head.

Winona's plan has to work. But if not, well, at least I'll go out swinging. She laughed at herself again and took one more hit for good measure.

CHAPTER 21

They reassembled in the hallway filled with body parts. The scene looked like the fever dream of a fifteen year old kid with a horror obsession who went by the username *HailSatan6969* online.

Delphine held her nunchucks, Mildred brandished a whip looking like Indiana Jone's great grandmother, and Gabe came limping from his room with a shotgun in one hand and a bottle of Wild Turkey being slid along the floor with his feet since his other arm was as useless as Kanye West at the Holocaust memorial.

But it was Winona that they all stared at. She didn't have a weapon. Instead, she had a book and a bag.

"WHAT YA GONNA DO? READ AND BORE HIM TO DEATH?" Gabe yelled.

Instead of responding, Winona emptied the bag on the floor. Salt, pouches with various herbs, some things that looked like bones, and some odds and ends landed at her feet. She looked at each of them.

"We cannot defeat the supernatural with weapons of the physical world. This is a spiritual battle", she said. As she examined the contents she bent down and picked something up, "Except for this. That's my mini vag massager. But the *rest* is for our battle against evil."

Mildred looked disappointed. She had used her whip for so many years. There were probably still bits of ass flesh from Henry Kissinger entwined in the leather.

Delphine stepped over to Winona. She put her hand on the other woman's shoulder. "I'm with you. Whatever happens, we fight together. And, live or die, we give this sonofabitch something to remember us by."

Gabe lowered his head, his shotgun resting at his side. "REMEMBER IN THAT BOOK BY STEPHEN KING, *IT*?"

Winona smiled at him, "Yes, I do. They fought together because they knew that was the *only* way to defeat Pennywise once and for all. They overcame obstacles, as a team, and waged the ultimate war. Not only for themselves but for the town as a whole. That's a beautiful thought, Gabe."

Gabe looked confused. "I MEAN THAT ONE SCENE WHERE THEY ALL BONED. LET'S DO THAT."

"*Shut up, Gabe*," they said in unison.

CHAPTER 22

Sheriff Bruce followed the blood trail outside of the emergency exit door. He was shaken, stirred, and blended but was determined to either find the survivors, subdue the killer, or die trying. He desperately hoped it wasn't the latter.

He rested his gun at his side and could hear his breathing sounding like an old pickup truck that didn't want to start. He kept his flashlight in his other hand toward the ground and eventually found himself at a service entrance. The door was unlocked so he let himself in.

The smell of dead flesh and fresh carnage assaulted his nose like cocaine did back in the eighties. He walked slowly, every squelch from his boots walking through blood being amplified.

In the distance, somewhere above, he heard voices. And unlike his week in Costa Rica experiencing ayahuasca, these voices were real. As he climbed the stairs he thought about what he would find at the top. *Certainly nothing good,* he figured. But what was good about *any* of this?

His department lay in ruins before him and body parts were more abundant than Molly at an underground rave. He trudged upward nevertheless, wishing he could just go home to his Asian porn and the sweet sweet taste of Natural Light.

He finally made it to the second floor and peered around the corner where the voices had originated.

It really shouldn't have surprised him that he'd see old people. This was an old folks home after all. But one woman had a whip that she seemed to be lovingly caressing, another had a pair of nunchucks, and one man had a shotgun and an arm that appeared to be bent like a dead tree in a hurricane.

But the other woman was on her knees, pouring salt from a container with that picture of a girl in a raincoat and umbrella on it, and making something from bones on the ground by her feet.

But the strangest thing was a black shadow that held the biggest knife he had ever seen. And it was headed for the survivors.

"Stop right there!" He shouted. The shadow did just that. It turned towards the sheriff and raced in his direction. Of all the times Bruce Gillis wanted to shoot some sumbitch for their crimes, this was the most exciting. He raised his pistol and aimed as the flying entity jettisoned forward, knife in hand. He pulled the trigger and unleashed hell.

CHAPTER 23

Winona was forming the boundaries between this evil, and her and her friends. The bones of her ancestors in the form of a protective spell, the salt circle, and just for good measure, some sage to surround it all.

When the gunshots rang out she fell as the bullets whizzed past her head. Gabe cried out, but whether in pain or just him being Gabe she didn't discern.

"WHAT THE HOLY FUCK", Gabe cried out. That answered her question. "HE SHOT ME".

Mildred was the first to extend her arms and run toward the sheriff. "Stop, help us!", she implored. The only answer she received was two bullets. One to her leg which caused her kneecap to bend backwards and the other to her head, a good amount of brain matter and skull fragments flying through the air in back of her. She collapsed into a pool of her own blood, her non-existent fingers pointing in front of her.

Delphine screamed and Gabe held his good hand against the side of his head where his ear, which was never good to begin with, was sheared clean off from the sheriff's bullets.

"Jesus H Christ", the sheriff exclaimed. He came from around the corner and surveyed the carnage before him. *Oh shit. Fuck fuck FUCK,* he thought. He walked to the group, his finger firmly on the outside of the trigger. "Is that you, Delphine?"

A shotgun blast exploded and sent him falling to the floor, the shot barely missing his head. "Don't shoot goddamnit."

"YOU SHOT FIRST', a voice yelled back. Gabe had managed to fire the shotgun, injuring his good shoulder in the process.

The sheriff lay on his belly and put his weapon on the ground. "Shit fire, Gabe. I'm here to help ya."

Gabe looked at him and lowered his shotgun even though the sheriff looked like some guy that had once beaten him just because he could.

That's when the shadow attacked.

It turned on the sheriff and the knife plunged into him to the hilt. Before he could say anything, the shadow twisted and, with a supernatural upward force, sliced through the sheriff from gut to throat. Meaty plops could be heard as his organs fell to the ground. A gurgle escaped his lips before his body fell unceremoniously on to his own insides.

Delphine shrieked, Gabe mumbled, and Winona kept at her task in hand.

Gabe and Delphine stood frozen. Winona hurriedly arranged the items on the ground. The shadow turned from the gutted body of the sheriff and looked at the trio, knife raised and moving toward them.

"Uhhhh, I hope you know what you're doing", Delphine said to Winona, "and you better make it fast".

Winona barely paid attention as she put the final pieces in place. Now it would come down to the words she spoke. The protection spell had to be spoken correctly in order for it to work. If not, her and the others would be human confetti.

"Delphine, Gabe, get inside the circle. Whatever you do, don't step outside of it", she ordered. Delphine was already there, by her side. Gabe had picked up the bottle of whiskey and took a big pull, smacking his lips in pleasure. He gingerly limped over to the women.

The shadow floated faster, anticipating the slaughter to come. The spirit of Dennis Forth laughed and gloated. *I will finally have my revenge. They took our sacred pagan grounds and built a retirement home. Not even a Starbucks but a place to house old people! But now it shall be mine again. I will raise our people up again and our sacrifices shall obtain the ears of the gods. And also build a no kill animal shelter. We're not* completely *heartless.*

Winona had less than a minute. She opened her spell book and started reciting the words on the page.

"A half cup of sugar
Two tablespoons of vanilla extract
Three eggs, beaten...."

She realized this page was an old family recipe. Delphine and Gabe were yelling, time was almost up. She turned the page and found what she needed. She cleared her throat, spit out an impressive loogy and recited.

The shadow was inches away, it's bloodlust permeating the air around it.

"May this circle be protected by the mercy of the saints. May no harm befall those within its radius. Evil has no place in here. May the foul and wicked be turned away. Praise to the goddess."

The shadow screamed and lunged. Delphine covered her head and yelped, Winona looked up from her book and stared wide eyed at the creature in front of them. Gabe took another swig and belched. He was turned in the wrong direction and didn't know what was going on.

The shadow plunged the knife downward, straight for Winona's head. She closed her eyes, accepting her failure.

Time seemed to go on for eternity. When she slowly opened her eyes, what she saw sent a relief through her so strong that she almost wet her Depends.

The creature was stabbing and slicing at them but coming up short. There wasn't a wall, and there weren't any sounds of metal scraping against a solid object. The knife just stopped short every time, seeming to be hitting something solid. The shadow grew frustrated and doubled it's efforts, raising and plunging the knife again and again as the three survivors stood protected.

Delphine had a look of pure amazement. Either that or a stroke. Gabe finally turned around and jumped back at what he saw. "WHAT THE HELL IS THAT?" He bellowed.

"It's been here the whole time, Gabe. What do you think we're all doing here?" Delphine asked.

Gabe just shrugged and took another drink.

As they watched in horror and fascination, the thing lifted its head and howled in anger. The noise shook the ground and bounced off the walls creating a cacophony of ear piercing noise.

Delphine and Winona held their hands tightly against their ears. Gabe looked at them in confusion. He never heard that well to begin with but now that his good ear was blown off, everything became a low mumble to him. *At least I still got my dick*, he thought with a smile.

Just as suddenly as it started, the noise stopped. Everything went completely silent. They all looked at one another, not sure what to do next.

"It worked, Winona, you saved our lives", Delphine took Winona's hands in hers and gave them a gentle squeeze. "I don't know how I'll ever repay you."

Winona gave her a smile, "Your friendship is payment enough."

"HOW ABOUT AN ORGY?"

"Shut up, Gabe", the women said in unison.

CHAPTER 24

They stayed in the protective circle just in case the demon, creature, shadow figure, whatever it was, came back. They'd come this far and were determined to make it out alive even if they had no idea of exactly how they would do that.

"Do you think it's gone for good?" Delphine asked Winona. She didn't think it would be that easy. Some common household products and an old book didn't seem like a way to expel a demonic entity but, then again, Winona had also kept the bones of her ancestors hidden away for all these years so maybe that was something.

"No", Winona said, "I don't think we've banished it. I'm pretty sure it's just regrouping, maybe gathering it's energy, waiting for a good time to strike. The protective spell works for now but I have no idea how strong it will remain or for how long. According to my grandmother's ritual book, the way to send a spirit like this back to the void is to obtain something from it that's personal when it was once a living being."

"You mean like something it once owned?"

"Yes, a piece of its clothing, a diary page, or even bits of its hair or skin. Anything it was attached to when it lived. There's a burning ritual that we can perform that will trap its soul. But where would we get something like that here?" Winona was trying to think of something they could use. She knew Brookhaven had a basement level and, in the basement, were long lost things. Things from visitors, residents, and even some historical artifacts from when the building was first erected. There might be something down there that belonged to Dennis Forth but how would they know? And what if they were attacked on the way down to the bottom level?

"i'LL GO", Gabe said suddenly. The women looked at him, never knowing if he was speaking to them or to himself about an unrelated manner. He did that often. He faced Delphine and Winona with a look of either resolve or flatulence, "THE BASEMENT. I'LL GO DOWN THERE."

Winona shook her head, "You don't know what to look for. Do you think there's going to be something down there that says 'Dennis Forth' written on it?"

"OF COURSE THERE IS", Gabe said, "THERE'S ALL KINDS OF SHIT DOWN THERE, INCLUDING A FRUITY TOOTY LOOKING COAT WITH THE NAME 'D. FORTH' WRITTEN IN THE COLLAR."

Delphine and Winona looked at each other in surprise. Neither of them were really sure about this. After all, Gabe had been drinking, he had injuries that could indicate he was in shock, and leaving the circle could be a suicide mission. But what choice did they have? If all three decided to go none of them might live.

Winona stood as close to Gabe as she could without being knocked down from the smell of whiskey and blood, "You be careful now, sweetie. I'll get a candle and you go get that shirt."

"BAH, YOU DON'T NEED A HANDLE AND I DON'T HAVE TO TAKE A SHIT. WAIT HERE AND GET A CANDLE WHILE I GO GET THE SHIRT" With that, Gabe walked out of the circle and wobbled towards the stairs. He thought about grabbing the shotgun but didn't. It wouldn't do any good and that would've meant leaving the bottle behind. It was making important decisions like this that made Gabe consider himself a leader.

"Do you think he's going to make it?" Delphine asked as they watched their friend start descending the steps.

Winona shook her head and shrugged, "My hopes aren't high but he's all we've got. I'll light the candle and say the spell." She rummaged around in her bag. "Shit", she said, "I don't have a lighter."

Delphine had just relit her joint and gave the lighter to Winona, "I'm always prepared for a party, girlfriend."

CHAPTER 25

Gabe was having trouble walking. This wasn't anything new or out of the ordinary, of course, but with his ear blown to hell and one arm just a useless bloody appendige on that side of his body, he was having a more difficult time balancing himself. The stairs down were easy enough, gravity did most of the work, but coming back up would be an issue. That's if he even made it to the basement. He was determined to help his friends though. He wasn't the most politically correct or proper man in the world but he was loyal.

He was sweating by the time he made it down to the first floor. The door leading to the basement was tucked away on the far side. He knew this because he would often sneak down there to drink or play the horizontal bop with the ladies of Brookhaven. They liked him just fine and he felt the same. Him and Delphine had been down there a few times and he hoped they'd be down there a few more. If they weren't butchered and sliced like a pig's anus at a bologna factory.

Using the wall for support, being careful not to drop his bottle at the same time, he half walked and half lurched down the hallway. He began to think that maybe that thing was gone for good. He hadn't heard or seen anything thus far, although he wouldn't have heard a freight train with squealing brakes from ten feet behind him. Still, he knew he was going to make it. The door was just ten feet away and all he had to do was take ten more steps.

Nine more steps.

Eight more steps.

He stopped to take a drink.

Seven more steps.

Six, five, four...

A howling screech that rattled the windows came from behind him. He didn't hear it so much as felt it, the walls vibrating. He turned his head as quickly as possible, which wasn't quick at all, and saw the shadow creature floating quickly in his direction, which was very quick. *Well fuck me sideways until I look like a question mark,* he thought. He jerked himself forward, almost stumbling to the floor. The vibrations picked up in intensity. If Gabe had been able to hear, the pressure in his head would have caused him to fall face first in agony. *Luckily, I had my ear shot off,* was something Gabe never would consider thinking but that's exactly what he thought as his hand wrapped around the door handle that led to the basement.

Right behind him and just two feet away, the creature brung his knife up and slashed through the air in an overhand arc just as Gabe swung the door open, ducked, and slammed it behind him, the knife coming so close that even Gabe could hear the swoosh it made by his ear. He stood on the top step. He had to catch his breath but knew he couldn't just stand there.

If it's a ghost it can come through doors, and Gabe waited for that to happen. But all was silent for some reason. *Why didn't it just come right through? It could have had me dead and in little pieces by now.* A bit too drunk to consider further but not too drunk to realize how lucky he was, Gabe started descending the basement stairs.

He hit the light switch on the wall and fluorescent bulbs buzzed to life sending the shadows scattering. At the bottom, he turned left and then took a right down one of the three aisles designated for lost or unclaimed items. There were boxes full of junk from Brookhaven's history. Pants, shirts, bras, mismatched socks, porn magazines (lots of porn mags), dildoes, vibraters, and even a sex swing. *Probably Millie's,* he thought with regret. Regret that his friend had her brains blown out and also regret that he'd never get to use the sex swing.

At the end of the aisle he saw the box he was looking for. Simply labeled *Stuff from construction* Gabe knew it contained artifacts and statues from when this land belonged to the pagan group. He was always told they performed rituals in the woods while dancing around a fire naked but none of that interested him, except for the naked part of course. *A bunch of religious kooks.* He lifted the lid and dust floated into his face. He coughed and tried to wave it away. He took another long drink of whiskey before setting the bottle on the floor and reaching into the box.

Clay figures that looked like a first year art student's attempt at a sculpture, various bags made from fabric containing dirt from the land, herbs, and fish bones but smelled like what you think something like that would. He rooted around in the box until his fingers felt the fabric of a coat. He yanked it out. Sure enough, written on the inside of the collar was the name 'D. Forth'. The coat was made from a polyester blend of some sort and had a dull pinkish hue to it. It was decorated with what looked like Boy Scout badges but were actually for achievements made by this pagan cult.

First Blood Sacrifice
Advanced Geological Spell Casting
Leadership For Samhain Rituals

Gabe held the ugly piece of outerwear between his thumb and forefinger like a person would grab a mousetrap with a large, very UN-Mickey looking rodent leaking its guts from the metal jaw. He dropped it to the ground and stepped on it with one foot while he carefully crouched down on top of it so he could use his good-ish hand to grab the edge of one of the badges and give it a tug. Apparently they didn't give awards for sewing because the badge came off, springing its stitching, with hardly any effort at all.

His task completed, he stuffed the badge in his pocket, picked up his bottle and headed back to the stairs. Gabe figured that thing was waiting for him. He didn't know enough about these things to know why it hadn't passed through the door and hung him up by his intestines already but that didn't matter. Because if it was still upstairs, he didn't stand a chance of getting back with his prize. *Guess I'll find out.* Before he ascended, a poem came to his mind. Something that had given him inspiration and encouragement in the past. A poem that spoke to his old tired heart and soul.

Here's to drinking
And being merry
Pass me the bottle
And pop her cherry!

With a tear in his eye, Gabe started up the stairs.

26

Dennis Forth screamed in frustration. How was it possible that these three old farts were thwarting him at every turn? He should have been finished by now. Hell, the evil spirit he was inhabiting had killed an entire army of men in a matter of minutes at some point in its everlasting state. This should have been a piece of bloody cake in comparison.

He had to admit that little protection spell was clever. He didn't know the old gal had it in her. But now they were all trapped with nowhere else to go. The old man had wandered off and Dennis had barely missed taking his head clean off. But why couldn't he pass through that damn door? There was so much he didn't understand when he had first summoned this hell beast to allow him to take possession of it. Just like buying a new car and having it break down a mile from the dealership, this creature wasn't living up to his expectations.

He was soothed somewhat by the fact that spells, no matter how effective, always had an expiration. They didn't last forever and it took a whole hearted belief and energy for them to stay their course for any great length of time. He had nowhere else to be and nothing else to do so if they wanted to play a waiting game, he was prepared to do just that. Eventually, their spells would fizzle out like a campfire in a rainstorm and they'd have nowhere to go.

Should I wait for the ancient bastard to come back through that unpassable door? Or should I patiently wait with the wrinkley broads upstairs until that protection spell finally gives out? He pondered his decision and decided that he would have a better chance upstairs. The old man could just stay locked in and wait him out but those chicks were in the open. Maybe, even, he could taunt them and chip away at their belief until the protective walls came crumbling down faster than a Malaysian airliner.

    He floated up the hallway and hoped he was making the right decision. After all, this creature was simply a loan. He knew it had other things to attend to. Wars, famines, derailing commuter trains, and getting Republican right wing nutjobs elected kept this thing pretty busy. So onward he floated, bloody gruesome dreams dancing through his head.

CHAPTER 27

Delphine was worried about Winona. After Gabe had been gone for a while, Winona had lit the candle, picked up her book, sat cross legged on the floor, and started chanting something Delphine couldn't understand.

Now, Winona was shaking and starting to sweat as she rocked back and forth mumbling foreign words. She appeared to be struggling yet Delphine didn't know if she should try to help or not. If she did something to interrupt whatever Winona was doing, it could be bad for Gabe and themselves. It was obviously a spell of some type but Delphine knew nothing about these sorts of things and didn't understand how they were supposed to work. She was worried sick about both of her friends and felt helpless as they both were at least doing something to try and save their lives.

Winona let out a tired moan, her brows knit together in pain and concentration. Her entire body trembled as she rocked faster on the floor. With a final long exclamation, she fell to her side, breathing heavily, her book pressed tightly to her chest. Delphine dropped to her knees beside her and wrapped her arms around the other woman. She cradled her while whispering softly into her ear that everything was okay. It wasn't. It definitely was nowhere near okay but she figured Winona knew this more than anybody so, instead, she held her friend and cooed encouragement into her ear.

After a few very long seconds, Winona sat up. "I think I kept Gabe safe. My spell wouldn't allow the evil to pass through the basement door. But I'm afraid the spell is waning and I'm not sure if he'll make it back or not."

Delphine clasped her hands together into a knot of concern and worry. "We should go get him. Help him. We can take the candle and burn whatever from downstairs."

"It's not that easy I'm afraid", Winona said, "my spells are not meant to last long. And without the spiritual energy to bring them forth, they are nothing but words in a book. Meaningless. I am spent, Delphine. And either that thing is going to find a way through the door where Gabe is soon or this protective circle will be nothing but a circle of useless salt and old bones. We are all sitting ducks and I don't know what to do about it." With that, Winona leaned into Delphine and started crying.

CHAPTER 28

It's working. They're weak and getting more vulnerable by the second. Dennis floated up to the very edge of the circle. He vibrated in anticipation. In just a few more minutes their protection would be no more and he was very much looking forward to slicing off their limbs and shoving them into their pompous assholes.

He lifted his shadow arms, the viscera covered knife held in one ghastly hand. He plunged downward. The spell was still in place but he could feel it give. It was becoming weaker. He danced in front of the old birds, enjoying the looks of terror on their faces. He screamed and amused himself as his voice thrashed in their minds like a shark on a scoopful of chum.

He slashed at the circle again, the knife giving way another half inch. He could sense their concentration breaking apart. He gleefully writhed. The time was imminent. He was finally going to get his revenge after all these years and there was nothing they could do about it.

Delphine and Winona lay on the floor together, holding each other in their final moments. Winona was out of energy and they were all out of time. She only hoped Gabe could make it out somehow. *Don't come back upstairs, you old fuckbag, just get outside. Please, just run.* She didn't know if she even had the energy for that thought to get to Gabe but at least, in her dying moment, she had tried.

The blade struck at them again and again, each time coming closer and closer to where they lay. After each strike a blood curdling scream echoed off the walls directly into their minds. And then, they heard a pop, like a balloon at the end of a needle.

Winona looked at Delphine with frightened eyes. "It's gone. I love you, girl"

"I love you too." They held each other tighter and closed their eyes, awaiting the final slaughter.

Dennis also heard the slight pop and he froze for just a couple of seconds. *This is it! Oh, I'm going to enjoy this very much.* He lifted the blade, prepared to strike one last time.

"FUCK YOUUUUUUU..." Gabe yelled, although yelling was just Gabe's normal tone. Neither the women nor Dennis had been paying any attention. At the sound of Gabe's bellow, Dennis turned quickly. Gabe was running (in the slowest snail like way possible but running nevertheless) right at him. He was grunting and wheezing but he kept coming straight at the creature.

"Gabe, watch out!" both women yelled in unison.

Dennis floated towards Gabe, knife at the ready. When Gabe was just inches away, Dennis slashed forward with his supernatural strength, looking forward to the squishing noises that would soon be coming from Gabe's flesh.

At the last possible second, Gabe did the unthinkable. He let himself fall to his side and slid underneath the thing's blade. It played out in slow motion because it was more like slow motion than actual full speed, but Gabe had enough momentum to pass through Dennis and finish his baseball slide inside of the circle.

The women looked at him, amazed. They reached out to grab him but he waved them off and held out his hand. Inside was what looked like a boy scout badge.

"BURN IT! WE DON'T NEED NO WATER, LET THE MOTHERFUCKER BURN."

Winona grabbed the badge. She had already lit the candle. But the shadow turned and was on them almost instantly. Gabe and Winona covered their heads for some kind of protection. Before Dennis could deliver the pain, Delphine stood.

"May this circle be protected by the mercy of the saints. May no harm befall those within it's radius. Evil has no place in here. May the foul and wicked be turned away. Praise to the goddess."

Dennis shrieked as his knife stopped short of his targets as if a physical wall had just dropped in front of them. Winona looked up at Delphine who held the spell book and was visibly shaking.

Delphine noticed her friends gawking at her incredulously. "What?" she said "It's all about belief and faith. Now let's end this sack of demonic shit once and for all."

Winona smiled and put the badge over the flame. It didn't take long for it to catch and pretty soon the whole badge was in flames, burning away at their feet. Dennis knifed and swung and kicked at them but the protection spell held firm. As he watched helplessly, his badge turned to ashes. As it did, he felt himself forcefully pulled from below. Not below the floor or the ground but from somewhere much further and deeper. A place that didn't belong to the natural world.

He clawed desperately to find purchase but there was none to be had. As he sank out of sight one final scream escaped his ghostly mouth. The building started vibrating then quickly shook at its very foundation. The walls rocked back and forth as pieces of the ceiling first trickled and then rained down around Gabe, Winona, and Delphine.

"We have to go. Now! Grab Gabe's waist." Delphine put his good arm around her shoulder and dragged him to his feet. Winona locked her arms around his waist to help support his weight. His other arm looked like a child's action figure in a microwave.

As the building started to buckle and collapse around them, the trio just kept moving. One foot in front of the other. There was no time to plan and nowhere else to go. They stumbled and limped their way downstairs and made a beeline for the front doors. Just as they stepped off the bottom step the second floor above started washing down metal, concrete, and glass all around them. They were getting cut from the bits that landed on their skin but they continued to their goal. The ground right ahead of them splintered in a zig zag line and spread like Delphine's varicose veins under their feet. The floor felt oddly spongy.

They glanced at each other and without saying a word, they all doubled down on their effort. The floor was shaking and, behind them, great crashing sounds echoed. The front doors were bent out of shape and more crooked than Gabe's back. The ground started opening up, swallowing everything in its path.

Delphine let go of Gabe's arm, reached behind her back, and pulled out her nunchucks that she had stuffed down the back of her pants. With a swing and a flourish that would make Bruce Lee smile, she swung at the glass and it shattered in a rain of glass. Brushing away the shards from the frame, she hooked Gabe's arm once again and, together, they walked out of Brookhaven just as the building collapsed in on itself with a roar. Fire exploded from the rubble as they barely escaped to safety.

CHAPTER 29

Ambulances, Fire Trucks, news vans, and Police vehicles from the surrounding counties gathered at the scene. The paramedics wrapped blankets around Delphine, Gabe, and Winona. Questions surrounded the chaos as reporters all groveled to get an exclusive from the survivors. The police also had questions, which would never be fully answered, but for now they could wait.

Before being led to separate ambulances, the three huddled together and stared at the carnage before them.

"I don't know where to go from here." Delphine sadly said. "Brookhaven has been my only home for so long and I don't have anybody else to stay with."

Winona grabbed her hand, "We'll figure something out, sweetie."

"YOU CAN STAY WITH ME." Gabe blurted out. The women turned their heads his way.

"You have a house?" Delphine asked.

Gabe nodded, "ALL PAID FOR. A PLACE IN THE COUNTRY. LET MY GRANDSON LIVE THERE FOR A BIT BUT HE SET UP A METH LAB IN THE BASEMENT AND WON'T BE OUT OF PRISON FOR AT LEAST TEN YEARS. IT'S BIG ENOUGH AND PRETTY CLEAN. BUT I HAVE TO WARN YOU, IT MIGHT BE HAUNTED."

Winona and Delphine stared at each other and nodded at the same time. "I think we can handle a few ordinary ghosts. Thank you, Gabe." Winona rubbed his back.

As the fires were being attended to and people swarmed all around them, they felt at peace and knew everything was going to be okay in the end.

EPILOGUE

Dennis had failed. His demon was gone and now he was trapped in this endless void. *They were lucky this time. So goddamned lucky. They escaped.* As he floated in the black nothingness of his prison he still had hope. *Spells don't last forever. And when this one breaks and releases me, I know exactly where that wrinkly old asshat lives. I'll be back for them and, this time, I won't come alone.*

THE END

ABOUT THE AUTHOR

David Royce is an expat from the United States currently living in Cambodia. He's the author of three horror story collections, a slasher/comedy novella, and his debut horror novel, Prey For Salvation. In addition, he's written two non-fiction books about living in Cambodia. His stories have appeared in several anthologies. When he's not writing, you can find him reviewing horror books on his YouTube channel, Horror Reads. You can find him on social media as well.

Buy his books: http://www.ko-fi.com/ddcambodia/shop or on Amazon here https://www.amazon.com/stores/author/B0797LJJ9X

Horror Reads YouTube channel:
http://www.youtube.com/@HorrorReads
Twitter (X): @horror_reads
Instagram: @horrorreadsyt
Threads: @horrorreadsyt
Facebook: @readscared

Don't miss out!

Visit the website below and you can sign up to receive emails whenever David Royce publishes a new book. There's no charge and no obligation.

https://books2read.com/r/B-A-GLQSE-IABOH

Connecting independent readers to independent writers.

Also by David Royce

Tales Of Salvation
Prey For Salvation
Brookhaven
Nothing Will Ever Be Fine Again